James Sheridan Knowles

Lectures On Dramatic Literature

James Sheridan Knowles

Lectures On Dramatic Literature

ISBN/EAN: 9783741186493

Manufactured in Europe, USA, Canada, Australia, Japa

Cover: Foto ©Andreas Hilbeck / pixelio.de

Manufactured and distributed by brebook publishing software
(www.brebook.com)

James Sheridan Knowles

Lectures On Dramatic Literature

LECTURES ON DRAMATIC LITERATURE

BY JAMES SHERIDAN KNOWLES

(Never before published)

MACBETH

"*Shephera.* But what's this I was gaun to say? ou, ay!—heard ye
ever Knowles's lectures on dramatic poetry?
"*North.* I have; they are admirable, full of matter, elegantly written
and eloquently delivered. Knowles is a delightful fellow and a man of
true genius."

Noctes Ambrosianæ.

FRANCIS HARVEY

4 ST. JAMES'S STREET

LONDON

1875

CHISWICK PRESS:—PRINTED BY WHITTINGHAM AND WILKINS,
TOOKS COURT, CHANCERY LANE.

THE Lectures upon Dramatic Literature by James Sheridan Knowles, delivered more than forty years ago, have never been published.

A few presentation copies have lately been printed from the original MS. found in memorandum-books. The lectures are very fragmentary and piecemeal, skipping from book to book. Sometimes one book, serving also as a diary or pocket-tablet, contains portions of two or three different lectures, with only the subject matter to distinguish them. Mr. Sydney Wells Abbott, of the British Museum, has deciphered them and made a sequence of their contents.

The memorandum-books are now carefully preserved in morocco cases.

From these Lectures the following pages have been selected for publication at this time, when the production of Macbeth at the Lyceum Theatre is the theme of general interest in artistic and literary circles.

London, November, 1875.

MACBETH.

PART THE FIRST.

T O exemplify those features in the acting dramatic poem, which contribute mainly to its success, we shall have recourse to Shakespeare; from among those incomparable records which he has left us of his genius, we shall select the tragedy of "Macbeth," as one of the most felicitous in plot and execution. Of this play we shall examine the first act.

In the tragedy of "Macbeth," the historical and the romantic are blended with singular effect. The materials with which history has furnished Shakespeare, are extremely few: the success of Macbeth against the Norwegians, his murder of Duncan at the instigation of Lady Macbeth, his usurpation of the throne, and his

B

death by the hand of Macduff. Of these four incidents, which are however sufficiently favourable to unity and climax of action, consists the groundwork of this play. These are the only links of his plot for which Shakespeare is indebted to history, all the rest are his own. With those links to guide him, he could doubtless have constructed a sufficiently interesting chain of natural situations and events; but the opportunity, which the remote period of the history presented him with, of indulging in the marvellous and supernatural, was too tempting to an imagination like his, not to be profited by. Accordingly, the powers of the air, the mysterious, impalpable ministers that wait on nature's mischief, were summoned to his aid, and in all the potency of prophecy, illusion and charm, appeared at the invocation of the enchanter.

The great aim of the dramatist, so far as the success of the acting dramatic poem is concerned, should be to excite expectation, and to keep it up throughout. To effect the latter, every new stage of his action should present some new object of interest. His subject should be proposed as soon as possible, and from that moment he should never allow his plot to stand still. I have witnessed plays so wretchedly deficient in this respect, that a whole act has passed, without the audience having any idea what the author was about. How different is Shakespeare's management in this admirable play. Scarcely has the curtain risen when the story begins to unfold itself:

> " *1st Witch.* When shall we three meet again,
> In thunder, lightning, or in rain?
> *2nd Witch.* When the burly burly's done,
> When the battle's lost and won.
> *3rd Witch.* That will be ere set of sun.
> *1st Witch.* Where the place?
> *2nd Witch.*   Upon the heath.
> *3rd Witch.* There to meet with Macbeth.
> *1st Witch.* I come, Graymalkin.
> *2nd Witch.* Paddock calls.
> *3rd Witch.* Anon.
> *All.* Fair is foul, and foul is fair:
> Hover through the fog and filthy air."

Here is the hand of the incomparable master. Here, by a scene composed of about half-a-dozen lines, is our interest already strongly excited. There is not in the whole course of the drama beside, ancient or modern, an instance where so much is effected in so narrow a compass. We are at once upon the tiptoe of definite expectation. We exclaim to ourselves—" There's matter here!" Such personages do not busy themselves about nothing, nor can he have a common part to act who is the theme of their conversation, the subject of their solicitude.

This impression is improved in the second scene, in which we are partly enlightened as to the character of Macbeth, by the Sergeant and by Macduff, who successively describe his prowess to the King, and whose relation tends powerfully to exalt our opinion of the

importance of the hero, and to increase our anxiety to
see him.

The third scene opens—and opens as it ought—with
the witches, the purport of whose approaching interview
with Macbeth is clearly inferred from the dialogue which
precedes his entrance, and which thoroughly develops
the evil quality of the beings that have come to give
him meeting. I must here, however, protest against
the grotesque effect which is generally given to these
members of the *dramatis personæ.* It is equally a
violation of historical and poetical truth. What can
be more preposterous, than to represent an object of
terror, in such a manner as to produce something like
a laugh at its appearance? How the stage-director can
fall into such an error, with the thunder and lightning
themselves to admonish him, is inexplicable. The circumstances under which the witches appear, the work
they have in hand, the very description of their persons
by Banquo, suggest anything rather than a low-comedy
group. They are the presiding, directing spirits of
tragedy; they are the furies of Æschylus, whose appalling presence, we are told, frustrated the mother's long-
cherished hope, and strangled infancy with the strong
convulsions of terror. How emphatically does the
kindred genius of the artist reprove such management.
There you see them, as doubtless Shakespeare saw them
in the mirror of his fancy, embodied spirits, the ministers

of evil; unearthly, wild, blasted things to cower and feel troubled at; less welcome than the storm that brings them; creatures accurst, whose looks bespeak their errand; the traffickers in things forbid; abominable and unutterable.

Macbeth at length enters, and never did tragic hero enter with greater effect. Alexander in his car is nothing to him. He does not immediately perceive the witches—an instance of the subtle perception of Shakespeare, which allows nothing to escape it that can enhance the effect of the action. Another author would probably have brought him and them face to face at once, but Shakespeare turns the impatience of his audience to better account: he increases it, to render its gratification the greater. The remark of Macbeth, in this short interval, is in fine keeping. It most appropriately turns upon the atmospherical phenomena, that have been produced by the supernatural × agency of which he himself is the unconscious, yet ignorant, object. At length he sees them—not directly though, but through the instrumentality of Banquo. Another happy hit! Who does not feel obliged to Banquo for pointing them out to him? How finely, too, the wonder with which he must contemplate them is felt through the wonder of his friend.

Their greeting is sublime. It is at once their errand and their salutation. It is a beautiful example of that condensation, for which the dialogue of Shakespeare is conspicuous:—

"*1st Witch.* All hail, Macbeth! hail to thee, thane of Glamis!
2nd Witch. All hail, Macbeth! hail to thee, thane of Cawdor!
3rd Witch. All hail, Macbeth, that shalt be king hereafter."

Shakespeare effects a thing, with half the effort which
it would cost another author, while, at the same time,
he executes it a thousand times more felicitously.   In
this, as much as in anything else, does the Shakesperian
drama stand alone.   Observe, again, the management of
the master.   The effect of this salutation upon him who
is the object of it, is announced not by any word which
he himself breathes, but by the remark of his companion-
in-arms—

"Good sir, why do you start, and seem to fear
Things that do sound so fair?"

Macbeth cannot, dares not trust his utterance, but he
cannot refrain from betraying what he feels.   The remark
of Banquo is the officious tongue of Macbeth's thought:
it lays open his soul to you to the bottom, as the salutation
of the third witch falling upon Macbeth's ear, rouses the
slumbering demon within him, like a flash of lightning illu-
minating a cavern and revealing to you a startled monster
couching there.   How happily does Shakespeare here
bring in the questioning of the witches by Banquo, not
only to allow the other time to recover himself, but to
give him an early foretaste of the fruits of guilty ambition :—

> " I' the name of truth,
> Are ye fantastical, or that indeed
> Which outwardly ye show ?   My noble partner
> You greet with present grace, and great prediction
> Of noble having, and of royal hope,
> That he seems rapt withal ; to me you speak not :
> If you can look into the seeds of time,
> And say which grain will grow, and which will not,
> Speak then to me, who neither beg, nor fear,
> Your favours, nor your hate."

At length, Macbeth addresses the witches. He is stimulated to that act by their preparing to depart :—

> " Stay, you imperfect speakers, tell me more :
> By Sinel's death, I know, I am thane of Glamis ;
> But how of Cawdor ?   The thane of Cawdor lives,
> A prosperous gentleman ; and to be king
> Stands not within the prospect of belief,
> No more than to be Cawdor.   Say, from whence
> You owe this strange intelligence ? or why
> Upon this blasted heath you stop our way
> With such prophetic greeting ?—Speak, I charge you."
> [*Witches vanish.*

The abrupt vanishing of the witches—much as we join with Macbeth in wishing them to stay—is an instance of that master perception which knew how to husband an enjoyment for us. They go when they have accomplished their errand, the quickening of the evil seed that is to shoot up apace and flourish in baleful, irrepressible rankness. Here occurs one of those thoughts of Shakespeare which are peculiarly his own—

" *Ban.* The earth hath bubbles, as the water has,
And these are of them."

The witches have vanished; but their work goes on
in the partial fulfilment of their prediction, by the arrival
of Rosse and Angus, with the news of Macbeth's acces-
sion to the title of the revolted thane of Cawdor; which
intelligence supplies a new source of interest, in the effect
that it produces on Macbeth, developing still further the
spirit of the future traitor and regicide, and keeping our
attention upon the strain till the close of the scene.
Seldom is the conception of Shakespeare done justice to
in the acting of this scene. Judge what an effect this
communication must produce upon a man in the situation
of Macbeth. Recollect his start at the prophetic salutation of the third witch. Reflect upon the stamp of
authority which that salutation receives from the fulfilment of the second prophetic " All hail!" Conceive the
deep absorption of his soul. Would you not expect him
to be off his guard, to forget that the eyes of Rosse,
Angus, and Banquo are upon him, to be lost to the
consciousness of all external perception? Shakespeare
intended that he should be so; nor does he leave it to
be guessed by you. He sets it down in terms intel-
ligible, distinct, and positive. The immediate natural
action of a person who receives good news, the truth of
which he distrusts, is an exclamation of incredulity; that

incredulity removed, the next natural action in a man with self-possession is a tribute of thanks to the messenger, especially when both are upon the same footing in point of rank. Macbeth cannot believe that he is thane of Cawdor.

> " The thane of Cawdor lives : why do you dress me
> In borrow'd robes ?
>   *Ang.*   Who was the thane lives yet :
> But under heavy judgment bears that life
> Which he deserves to lose. Whether he was
> Combined with Norway ; or did line the rebel
> With hidden help and vantage : or that with both
> He laboured in his country's wreck, I know not ;
> But treasons capital, confessed and proved,
> Have overthrown him."

All ground of doubt is removed. There stand Rosse and Angus to receive the tribute which courtesy and gratitude award them. Does Macbeth render it? No, he overlooks both them and their news in gloating upon the crown which infallible prophecy has placed upon his head.

> " Glamis, and thane of Cawdor :
> The greatest is behind."

He suddenly recollects himself. He finds he has been forgetful. He repairs his error

> " Thanks for your pains."

But more than this. He fears that his abstraction may

c

have been perceived by Banquo—Banquo who heard the prediction of the witches—Banquo who saw him start when the name of king was put upon him—Banquo whose sagacity may penetrate the guilty cause of his absence of mind. Banquo's thought must be made to look another way. Macbeth must seem to have been occupied by anything but the reflections that have been actually passing within him.

> " Do you not hope your children shall be kings,
> When those that gave the thane of Cawdor to me,
> Promised no less to them ? "

Banquo, free from suspicion, replies :—

> " That, trusted home,
> Might yet enkindle you unto the crown,
> Besides the thane of Cawdor. But 'tis strange :
> And oftentimes, to win us to our harm,
> The instruments of darkness tell us truths ;
> Win us with honest trifles, to betray us
> In deepest consequence."

Macbeth does not hear a word of this. He is abstracted again. He scarcely recovers his self-possession ere he relapses. Ask him what Banquo has just been saying to him, he will be as—as if Banquo had not spoken at all. Do you doubt it? Why, he is utterly unconscious that his friend has taken Rosse and Angus apart to confer with them.

What business has this line here if Macbeth is aware

of what has just been passing? Why interrupt his own
meditations, and intrude upon the private conversation of his
friends for the now superfluous purpose of thanking Rosse
and Angus, unless because he has relapsed,—becomes suddenly conscious of his abstraction,—is unconscious of his
being at liberty to indulge in it, and from the recollection
of his having committed one error is apprehensive of
being guilty of a second? I have seen some of our first-
rate actors leisurely turn round and address their thanks
to Rosse and Angus standing at the back of the stage,
thus obliterating as it were one of the finest traits of the
scenic picture. No, Macbeth believes Rosse and Angus
to be still standing on the spot where first he saw them;
he has become thoroughly abstracted again; he suddenly
recovers his recollection; hastens to repair a breach of
decorum of which he suspects himself to have been guilty,
supposing Rosse and Angus to be standing where last he
saw them; turns to do it; finds they have removed to a
distance with Banquo, and then resumes the former train
of his thought.

The scene changes. From what we perceive of Macbeth when he is first introduced to us, he is evidently a
man whose nature is not exactly attempered to the commission of crime. He can admit the thought of the
murder, but he cannot entertain it without shuddering.
He wants provocation to nerve his hand for the dagger,
and Shakespeare finds it for him in this scene in the

advancement of Duncan's eldest son to the principality of
Cumberland. The interest of this scene is still further
enhanced by Duncan's announcing his intention to visit
Macbeth's castle, thus presenting, as it were, to Macbeth
the opportunity for despatching him.

" SCENE IV.—*Forres.   A Room in the.Palace.*

Flourish, Enter DUNCAN, MALCOLM, DONALBAIN, LENOX, *and* Attendants.

Dun. Is execution done on Cawdor ?   Are not
Those in commission yet returned ?
Mal.   My liege,
They are not yet come back.   But I have spoke
With one that saw him die :· who did report,
That very frankly he confessed his treasons ;
Implored your highness' pardon ; and set forth
A deep repentance ; nothing in his life
Became him like the leaving it ; he died
As one that had been studied in his death,
To throw away the dearest thing he owed,
As 'twere a careless trifle.
Dun.   There's no art
To find the mind's construction in the face :
He was a gentleman on whom I built
An absolute trust.   O worthiest cousin !

Enter MACBETH, BANQUO, ROSSE, *and* ANGUS.

The sin of my ingratitude even now
Was heavy on me ; thou art so far before,
That swiftest wing of recompense is slow
To overtake thee.   Would thou hadst less deserved,
That the proportion both of thanks and payment
Might have been mine !   Only I have left to say,
More is thy due than more than all can pay.
Macb. The service and the loyalty I owe,
In doing it, pays itself.   Your highness' part

Is to receive our duties : and our duties
Are to your throne and state, children and servants ;
Which do but what they should, by doing every thing
Safe toward your love and honour.
    Dun.   Welcome hither :
I have begun to plant thee, and will labour
To make thee full of growing. Noble Banquo,
That hast no less deserved, nor must be known
No less to have done so ; let me enfold thee,
And hold thee to my heart.
    Ban.   There if I grow,
The harvest is your own.
    Dun.   My plenteous joys
Wanton in fulness, seek to hide themselves
In drops of sorrow.——Sons, kinsmen, thanes,
And you whose places are the nearest, know,
We will establish our estate upon
Our eldest, Malcolm ; whom we name hereafter
The Prince of Cumberland : which honour must
Not, unaccompanied, invest him only,
But signs of nobleness, like stars, shall shine
On all deservers.——From hence to Inverness,
And bind us further to you.
    Macb. The rest is labour, which is not used for you :
I'll be myself the harbinger, and make joyful
The hearing of my wife with your approach ;
So, humbly take my leave.
    Dun.   My worthy Cawdor !"

Here the exit speech of Macbeth admirably describes
his settled purpose, and the degree in which his nature
recoils at the idea of carrying that purpose into execution :—

    " The Prince. of Cumberland !—That is a step,
On which I must fall down, or else o'er-leap,
For in my way it lies. Stars, hide your fires !

> Let not light see my black and deep desires:
> The eye wink at the hand! yet let that be,
> Which the eye fears, when it is done, to see."

We cannot take our leave of this scene without pointing out an instance of that perfect self-identification with his characters, in which Shakespeare leaves every other dramatist so far behind him. I allude to the different manners in which Macbeth and Banquo respectively acknowledge the gracious reception given them by the King. The reply of the latter comes from the heart, is brief and effortless, breathing the workings of an honest and grateful nature overpowered by excessive kindness; while that of the former comes from the head alone, is a tissue of fine-spun reasoning upon an obvious proposition —in a word, the speech of a man who is conscious of a false heart, and feels the necessity of masking it with as fair a face as possible.

The historical fact, that Macbeth was instigated by his wife to murder Duncan, suggested to Shakespeare the character of Lady Macbeth. From this single trait, he inferred the whole of a character, for fidelity of keeping and force, if not superior to any, at least inferior to none in the wide range of his immortal drama. Here he has, indeed, realized the highest feat of the terrible in romance, by embodying the spirit of a fiend in a human form ;—a being composed of flesh and blood, and not without the sympathies which result from the living union of such ingredients, but possessing them in utter subserviency to the presiding evil principle; susceptible of conjugal attachment, yet reckless of sacrificing the honour, the virtue, the peace of her husband to the gratification of her own ambition; no stranger to the instinct that links the parent to her offspring, yet capable of conceiving and supporting the idea of the babe that milks her, at one moment smiling at her breast, and the next a corpse upon the ground, its brains dashed out by her own hand; a daughter too, but the filial knot availing only to awaken a momentary compunction from the effects of which no sooner does she recover, than she is if possible twice the demon that she was before. She takes no more account of blood, than if it were water. That from the sight of which unused nature instinctively recoils, though shed for a salutary purpose, under circumstances the most revolting, only serves to furnish her with an image of pleasure—

> " If he do bleed,
> I'll gild the faces of the grooms withal."

She does so, and never hastens to wipe her hands, but brings them reeking, to taunt her pale and quaking husband with their colour. This is a character, our feeling of the masterly conceptions and delineations of which must ever transcend any attempt to describe it. It was a theme every way worthy the genius of Shakespeare, and fully did that genius prove that it was equal to the task. Shakespeare doubtless saw the want of such an accomplice, to spur the resolution of a man—a gallant, generous soldier, who had much that was noble in him despite his vaulting ambition. And such has Shakespeare drawn him. A man alive to the claims of moral duty:—

> " He's here in double trust :
> First, as I am his kinsman and his subject,
> Strong both against the deed ; then, as his host,
> Who should against his murderer shut the door,
> Not bear the knife myself."

Jealous of honour :—

> " He hath honoured me of late ; and I have bought
> Golden opinions from all sorts of people,
> Which would be worn now in their newest gloss,
> Not cast aside so soon."

Who can conceive and appreciate the beauty of virtue :—

> " Besides, this Duncan
> Hath borne his faculties so meek, hath been
> So clear in his great office, that his virtues
> Will plead like angels, trumpet-tongued, against
> The deep damnation of his taking off."

Who has a thought of heaven :—

> " But, in these cases,
> We still have judgment here ; that we but teach
> Bloody instructions, which being taught, return
> To plague the inventor."

and who has much of the milk of human kindness :—
Act ii. Sc. ii
Act v Sc. iii
Act v Sc V

I say the assistance of such an accomplice was necessary to confirm the bloody purpose in such a man; to
screw up his courage to the sticking place, and keep it
there.

This extraordinary creation of the bard is introduced
to us in the fifth scene, and awakens a new interest; but
at the same time all is perfectly in keeping. She enters
reading a letter from Macbeth, communicating the extraordinary encounter he has had, the predictions he has
heard, and the partial fulfilment of those predictions.

But who that remembers the stage, some twenty years
ago, can ever revert to this letter without associating with
it the idea of the tongue that used to read it, as it was
universally allowed it had never been read before, and
may almost be allowed it never will be read again? What
a specimen of histrionic art was the reading of that letter!
the figure, the action, the eye, the tone,—such a com-
bination as one would be tempted to deny that Nature
could surpass, and to doubt if she could repeat. One
would almost think as soon of looking for another Shakespeare, as looking for another Siddons. Years have
passed since her retirement from the stage. Candidate
after candidate has presented herself; but in the peculiar
walk of that actress—the towering of tragedy—in whom
have we acknowledged her successor? When we, who
saw her, look back upon the acting of that empress
of her art; while we thrill with the bare recollection

D

of what her genius could achieve; while we ask ourselves what would we not give to witness its workings
again; does the faintest hope arise to our minds that we
shall ever hear the characters of Elvira, Zara, Volumnia,
Queen Catherine, and Lady Macbeth alluded to, and
associate with them the personation of any other actress?
With less of mannerism than her talented brother, she
possessed a thousand times the genius; her scenes—those
in which the characters she represented took the lead—
were one continuous flashing of intensely excited imagination; passion with her rose to the topmost pitch, but
never to offending, for it was genuine. It did not re-
semble the artificial storm got up by the artists of the
theatre; it was the tempest itself; it was the liquid sea
put into motion and chafed by the very winds of heaven,
and tossing and resounding amidst the thunders and lightnings of heaven. When her Elvira, about to be led out
to die, denounced Pizarro, you trembled for Pizarro, not
for Elvira.

Zara threatening Alphonso made palpable to you all
that you had ever heard or fancied of the fierce and
opposite extremes of passion;—how the same love that
now could make us feed another's life with our own, anon
could strangle its object. Her Volumnia was indeed the
Roman matron: it showed you the original of the historic
portrait, which it not only vindicated from the suspicion
of exaggeration, but even transcended. Her Queen

Cathcrine was the perfect embodying of conscious royalty,
her mere

"Lord Cardinal, to you I speak,"

brought Wolsey from his chair to her feet; while that
stateliness of soul, which instead of bending under wrong
and insult, only towered the more in the personation of
this inimitable actress, was felt by the audience no less in
their own perception, than in the effect which it produces
upon the voluptuous tyrant whose barbarity puts it to the
test. But the Lady Macbeth of Mrs. Siddons was her
masterpiece. Not that she was not equally happy in her
conception of other characters, but that here her fine
genius had greater scope for its development; and here
what terms of eulogy are rich enough to sum up the
amount of her merits?

The Lady Macbeth of Mrs. Siddons was the Genius of
guilty ambition personified;—express in form, in feature,
motion, speech. An awe invested her. You felt as if
there was a consciousness in the very atmosphere that
surrounded her, which communicated its thrill to you.
There was something absolutely subduing in her presence
—an overpowering something, that commanded silence;
or if you spoke, prevented you from speaking above
your breath. It was a thing, once witnessed, never
to be forgotten, more to be remembered than the most
gorgeous pageant that ever signalized the triumph of

human pride, or fulfilled the imaginings of human admiration.

> "They met me in the day of success; and I have learned by the per-
> fectest report, they have more in them than mortal knowledge. When I
> burned in desire to question them further, they made themselves—air."

In the look and tone with which she delivered that word,
you recognized ten times the wonder with which Macbeth
and Banquo actually beheld the vanishing of the witches.

> "Whiles I stood rapt in the wonder of it, came missives from the King,
> who all-hailed me 'Thane of Cawdor;' by which title, before, these weird
> sisters saluted me, and referred me to the coming on of time, with 'Hail,
> King that shalt be!'"

The expression which she gave to the delivery of the
word "King" in this sentence was such, that it needed
not her tongue to tell you of the dagger which was destined
to be sheathed in the heart of Duncan. But 'tis im-
possible to indulge in minute criticism. Were we to do
so, we could occupy, in the description of Mrs. Siddons's
Lady Macbeth, as many lectures as have been comprised
in the entire course; and after all, we should remain
unsatisfied with ourselves. Her acting in the scene
where she reproves her vacillating husband, and absolutely shames him into resolution; her acting in the
scene where the murder is perpetrated, where with un-
hesitating, collected step she enters the chamber of blood,

to replace the daggers of the grooms, and as calmly issues
from it again as if she had but newly lifted her head from
the pillow of innocent sleep; her acting in the banquet-
scene where the self-possession of Lady Macbeth is put
to the severest trial—when by the disturbed, distempered
conscience of her feeble husband she is placed upon the
brink of a precipíce, and stands there as cool as if the
airy void before her were firm as the solid footing whence
she surveys it; her acting in these scenes, were things no
more to be embodied in description than the speed and
brightness of the lightning flash, which nothing can give
you a conception of except the lightning. The reproof of
her scorn was blasting. Though Macbeth's resolution to
proceed no further in the business, had been fifty times
as strong as it was, it must have crouched before her;
and he must have gone on, though a hundred Duncans
stood in his way.

But the sleeping scene, where she walks and dreams!
I could pity a murderess who should look upon that
scene. The ghostly group that enter the tent and
surround the couch of Richard, bring with them not
the tithe of the horror that attends that silent woman,
Lady Macbeth walking in her sleep. Though pit, gallery,
and boxes were crowded to suffocation, the chill of the
grave seemed about you while you looked on her;—there
was the hush and the damp of the charnel-house at
midnight; you had a feeling as if you and the medical

attendant, and lady-in-waiting, were alone with her; your flesh crept and your breathing became uneasy; you felt the tenaciousness of the spot which she was trying to rub out upon her hand; the scent of blood became palpable to you; while the sigh of her remorse seemed to ascend from an unfathomable abyss of misery and despair.

We return to the fifth scene. The reading of Macbeth's letter is followed by a soliloquy where his character is briefly but admirably sketched, while that of Lady Macbeth begins to develop itself.

> " Glamis thou art, and Cawdor; and shalt be
> What thou art promised :—yet, do I fear thy nature ;
> It is too full o' the milk of human kindness,
> To catch the nearest way : Thou wouldst be great,
> Art not without ambition ; but without
> The illness should attend it.   What thou wouldst highly,
> That wouldst thou holily ; wouldst not play false,
> And yet wouldst wrongly win : thou'dst have, great Glamis,
> That which cries, ' Thus thou must do, if thou have it :
> And that which rather thou dost fear to do,
> Than wishest should be undone.'   Hie thee hither,
> That I may pour my spirits in thine ear,
> And chastise, with the valour of my tongue,
> All that impedes thee from the golden round,
> Which fate and metaphysical aid doth seem
> To have thee crowned withal."

The announcement of the King's approaching visit reveals her fully in the most appalling adjuration that was ever breathed by human lips.

" Come you spirits
That tend on mortal thoughts, unsex me here ;
And fill me, from the crown to the toe, top-full
Of direst cruelty ! make thick my blood,
Stop up the access and passage to remorse ;
That no compunctious visitings of nature
Shake my fell purpose, nor keep peace between
The effect aud it ! Come to my woman's breasts,
And take my milk for gall, you murdering ministers,
Wherever in your sightless substances
You wait on nature's mischief ! Come, thick night,
And pall thee in the dunnest smoke of hell !
That my keen knife see not the wound it makes ;
Nor heaven peep through the blanket of the dark
To cry, ' Hold, hold ! ' "

The arrival of Macbeth forms the last incident of
this scene, bringing us to a further and more interesting
stage of the action, in the avowal of Lady Macbeth's
determination to have the murder of her confiding guest
and monarch perpetrated under her own roof.

We come to the sixth scene, which has been instanced
by a celebrated artist and critic—Sir Joshua Reynolds—
as an example of relief, analogous to what is technically
called repose in painting. The artist and critic I allude
to considers this to be the effect of design on the part of
Shakespeare—that it is intended by him to relax the
tension, the extreme tension of that interest which has
been hitherto excited in the audience, and kept constantly
upon the strain. Notwithstanding the eloquence of the
remark, and the ingenuity with which it is enforced, I am

inclined to take a different view of the subject, and to consider this scene as another and a higher step in the climax of the action. That Duncan should contemplate with satisfaction the pleasant seat of Macbeth's castle, and that Banquo should participate in the feelings of the King, are perfectly natural; but that the audience should partake this view, is as preposterous as to suppose that we could see a man about to step into a cavern which we know to be the den of a wild beast, and participate in his admiration of the foliage which might happen to adorn its entrance. So far, if I mistake not, from there being any relaxing of the interest here, there is an absolute straining of it. The unconsciousness of the destined victim to the fate that awaited it, the smiling flowers that dressed it, and its playful motions as it walked to the altar of sacrifice must have served, not to assuage, but to aggravate in the beholder the feeling of its predicament. There is no relief—no repose here. How often in witnessing this scene have I felt a wish that some suspicion of foul play would flash across the mind of Banquo, and that he would hang upon the robes of the king and implore him not to enter.

Here again we perceive that fine keeping of character which distinguishes all the portraits of Shakespeare. Whom does he send to receive? Not Macbeth; not the man who cannot meditate a damning deed and look up clear—who alters favour: but her who could at once, and while con-

scious nature shuddered all around her, remain imperturb-
able as the weapon in her hand.

The closing scene of this act is a higher point of the
climax still: the last debate as to innocence and crime.
It commences with the soliloquy of Macbeth, which I
confess I have seldom heard spoken with that perturbation
which appears to me to suit it. The manner in which
this soliloquy is generally delivered reminds me of the
seaman who is accustomed to the gale, and sits cool and
collected at the helm, though at every yard there yawns
a grave before him. I would have it an entirely different
thing. Macbeth is no such seaman. There should be
infinite discomfiture and confusion in it. It should be
delivered by fits and starts. I would attempt to give a
reading of it did I not know that conception and execution
are different things. The one is the soul and the other
the body, and the body does not always correspond to the
soul. This soliloquy is in fine keeping with the character
of Macbeth, and furnishes rich groundwork for the dialogue which immediately follows between him and Lady
Macbeth, and which advances the action to another stage
—that where the murder of Duncan is eventually deter-
mined upon.

E

PART THE SECOND.

NEVER had dramatist the art of enhancing the effect of a crisis or capital incident or situation, as Shakespeare had. A brief review of the first act of "Macbeth" will serve to establish this fact.

The act consists of seven scenes, each succeeding one of which increases in interest, and all of which bear upon one and the same argument—the guilty ambition of the hero.

The first scene announces Macbeth in the brief, pregnant dialogue of the weird sisters. An extraordinary scene, consisting of ten irregular four-feet lines, yet full of power, begetting a lively interest, perfect in keeping, everything congenial to the work in hand, the time, the place, the circumstances.

The time,—at set of sun :—

> " When the hurly burly's done,
> When the battle's lost and won."

The place,—the heath, the abode of savage sterility and solitude. The circumstances,—thunder, lightning or rain. See how subtly he awakens the feeling most congenial to his theme. We cower and draw together, and ask ourselves what is to come.

The second scene is the hall of majesty; but thither, though unseen, do the witches accompany us, for there we hear again of him whom they are to meet ere set of sun upon the heath, amid thunder, lightning or rain— Macbeth. Here we learn who and what the hero is,— the renowned champion of his king and of his country. He is described to us by his deeds; deeds of prowess almost superhuman. One single arm decides the multitudinous strife of blood, and it is his. The single arm of Macbeth! And what transpires here of paramount importance? One of the King's nobles—the Thane of Cawdor—proves a traitor. He is condemned to the block, and messengers are despatched to invest Macbeth with his forfeited title. Except for this preparatory step, one of the most striking incidents in the following scene would have been deprived of half its force. The fulfilment of the second witch's prophetic " All hail! " without it would have appeared a mere trick of the dramatist, whereas now it falls out naturally. 'Tis by such means, that of all dramatists Shakespeare comes the nearest to nature. 'Tis thus that he gives plausibility to nature. 'Tis thus that he gives plausibility even to the supernatural when he has occasion to resort to it. Mark the progress here. Mark the building of the climax.

In the first scene we inquire who Macbeth is: in the second we find it out—but only by report. We have to see him yet. We have to become personally acquainted with him; and accordingly the Heath opens upon us in the third scene with full effect. There it is, and there are the thunder and the lightning and the rain, and there are the witches, and they are welcome. But where is Macbeth, for the sake of whom they are so? Where is the man about whom we heard the weird sisters consult? —whose deeds of valour we have just heard recited to the king?—whom the king in gratitude has sent his servants to greet with the title of the revolted Thane of Cawdor? Where is he? Are you not impatient to see him? You are, and Shakespeare knows it; but he knows better than to let you see him yet. To introduce Macbeth now would be an obvious thing—a thing of course. No, he diverts your mind from the subject. He rivets your attention upon the witches themselves. He entangles you in a dialogue which takes place between them concerning a grudge which one of them owes to a sailor's

wife and means to repay; and when you are engrossed
in the examination of

> "the pilot's thumb,
> Wreck'd as homeward he did come,"

the drums of Macbeth startle you, and most gratefully
recall your attention to the object of paramount solicitude; that attention refreshed and invigorated by partial
diversion. Now for the drift of the mysterious, precon-
certed interview. How gradually and impressively it is
unfolded! Let us pause to contemplate the extraordinary
power of this scene, which for our own sakes we shall
allow to speak for itself.

Enter MACBETH *and* BANQUO.

Macb. So foul and fair a day I have not seen.
Ban. How far is't called to Forres?—What are these
So withered and so wild in their attire,
That look not like the inhabitants o' the earth,
And yet are on't? Live you? or are you aught
That man may question? You seem to understand me,
By each at once her choppy finger laying
Upon her skinny lips:—you should be women,
And yet your beards forbid me to interpret
That you are so.
  Macb.   Speak, if you can: what are you?
 1st Witch. All hail, Macbeth! hail to thee, thane of Glamis!
 2nd Witch. All hail, Macbeth! hail to thee, thane of Cawdor!
 3rd Witch. All hail, Macbeth! that shalt be king hereafter!
 Ban. Good sir, why do you start, and seem to fear
Things that do sound so fair? I' the name of truth
Are ye fantastical, or that indeed

Which outwardly ye show? My noble partner
You greet with present grace and great prediction
Of noble having, and of royal hope,
That he seems rapt withal. To me you speak not.
If you can look into the seeds of time,
And say, which grain will grow and which will not,
Speak then to me, who neither beg nor fear
Your favours nor your hate.
   1st Witch. Hail!
   2nd Witch. Hail!
   3rd Witch. Hail!
   1st Witch. Lesser than Macbeth, and greater.
   2nd Witch. Not so happy, yet much happier.
   3rd Witch. Thou shalt get kings, though thou be none.
So all hail! Macbeth and Banquo!
   1st Witch. Banquo and Macbeth, all hail!
   Macb. Stay, you imperfect speakers, tell me more:
By Sinel's death, I know, I am thane of Glamis;
But how of Cawdor? The thane of Cawdor lives,
A prosperous gentleman; and to be king
Stands not within the prospect of belief,
No more than to be Cawdor. Say, from whence
You owe this strange intelligence? or why
Upon this blasted heath you stop our way
With such prophetic greeting? Speak, I charge you. [*Witches vanish.*
   Ban. The earth hath bubbles, as the water has,
And these are of them. Whither are they vanished?
   Macb. Into the air, and what seemed corporal, melted
As breath into the wind.—Would they had stayed!
   Ban. Were such things here as we do speak about?
Or have we eaten of the insane root,
That takes the reason prisoner?
   Macb. Your children shall be kings.
   Ban. You shall be king.
   Macb. And thane of Cawdor too: went it not so?
   Ban. To the self-same tune and words. Who's here?

Enter ROSSE *and* ANGUS.

   Rosse. The king hath happily received, Macbeth,

The news of thy success; and when he reads
Thy personal venture in the rebel's fight,
His wonders and his praises do contend,
Which should be thine, or his : silenced with that,
In viewing o'er the rest o' the self-same day,
He finds thee in the stout Norweyan ranks ;
Nothing afeard of what thyself didst make,
Strange images of death.   As thick as tale,
Came post with post; and everyone did bear
Thy praises in his kingdom's great defence,
And poured them down before him.

   Ang.   We are sent
To give thee, from our royal master, thanks ;
To herald thee into his sight, not pay thee.

   Rosse. And, for an earnest of a greater honour,
He bade me, from him, call thee thane of Cawdor:
In which addition, hail, most worthy thane !
For it is thine.

   Ban.   What, can the devil speak true ?

   Macb. The thane of Cawdor lives.   Why do you dress me
In borrowed robes ?

   Ang.   Who was the thane lives yet :
But under heavy judgment bears that life
Which he deserves to lose.   Whether he was
Combined with Norway, or did line the rebel
With hidden help and vantage, or that with both
He laboured in his country's wreck, I know not;
But treasons capital, confessed and proved,
Have overthrown him.

   Macb. [*aside*] Glamis, and thane of Cawdor !
The greatest is behind.   [*To Rosse and Angus.*]
Thanks for your pains.

   [*To Ban.*] Do you not hope your children shall be kings,
When those that gave the thane of Cawdor to me
Promised no less to them ?

   Ban.   That, trusted home,
Might yet enkindle you unto the crown,
Besides the thane of Cawdor.   But 'tis strange :
And oftentimes, to win us to our harm,

The instruments of darkness tell us truths,
Win us with honest trifles, to betray us
In deepest consequence.
Cousins, a word, I pray you.
  Macb. [*aside.*]   Two truths are told,
As happy prologues to the swelling act
Of the imperial theme. I thank you, gentlemen.
[*Aside.*] This supernatural soliciting
Cannot be ill, cannot be good: if ill,
Why hath it given me earnest of success,
Commencing in a truth? I am thane of Cawdor:
If good, why do I yield to that suggestion
Whose horrid image doth unfix my hair,
And make my seated heart knock at my ribs,
Against the use of nature? Present fears
Are less than horrible imaginings:
My thought, whose murder yet is but fantastical,
Shakes so my single state of man, that function
Is smothered in surmise, and nothing is,
But what is not.
  Ban.   Look, how our partner's rapt.
  Macb. [*aside.*] If chance will have me king, why, chance may crown me
Without my stir.
  Ban.   New honours come upon him
Like our strange garments, cleave not to their mould
But with the aid of use.
  Macb. [*aside.*]   Come what come may,
Time and the hour runs through the roughest day.
  Ban. Worthy Macbeth, we stay upon your leisure.
  Macb. Give me your favour: my dull brain was wrought
With things forgotten. Kind gentlemen, your pains
Are registered where every day I turn
The leaf to read them. Let us toward the king.—
Think upon what hath chanced; and, at more time,
The interim having weighed it, let us speak
Our free hearts each to other.
  Ban.   Very gladly.
  Macb. Till then, enough. Come, friends."

You mark the regular progression here. Everything occurs in its proper time and place, gradually increasing in importance until the interest attains to a high pitch of intensity. First, the object of the witches in seeking this interview with Macbeth—revealed dimly, but not the less impressively on that account; secondly, the new argument set before you in their prophecies with regard to Banquo, which you feel assured they do not idly contrast with those that affect Macbeth; thirdly, Macbeth's discredit of the second prophetic "All hail!" showing you that he is yet ignorant of his new good fortune, and giving increased importance to the incident that confers it; fourthly, the mysterious vanishing of the witches, just when you hope with Macbeth that they are going to tell him more; fifthly,·the arrival of the messengers, whom in the preceding scene you saw despatched by the king to salute Macbeth with the title that has so unexpectedly fallen to him. How you long for them to speak! How you anticipate the astonishment of Macbeth! Sixthly and lastly, the effect of their communication, developing the thoughts and feelings of the future regicide and usurper. How you enjoy his abstraction, his return to recollection, his relapse, his recovery again, his efforts to excuse himself, and to prevent Banquo from suspecting the cause which—

> " Shakes so my single state of man, that function
> Is smothered in surmise ; and nothing is,
> But what is not."

F

In the fourth scene we find the climax still ascending.
The action consists of an interview between the King
and his sons, his nobles, and subsequently Macbeth and
Banquo. The interest here is heightened by the King's
announcement of his intention of visiting Macbeth's castle.
The victim of his own ambition, and of the evil agency
which called it into activity, reveals himself less question-
ably here. He precedes the King, to announce to Lady
Macbeth the high honour that awaits her. The King's
eldest son, Malcolm, has just been nominated the successor
to the crown, by being promoted to the dignity of Prince
of Cumberland. Action and promptness must now take
place of delay and hesitation. The die is almost cast.
Macbeth exclaims to himself, as he repairs to execute the
gracious errand of the king,—

> " The Prince of Cumberland !   That is a step,
> On which I must fall down, or else o'erleap ;
> For in my way it lies," &c.

The fifth scene opens. What is the climax of action
now? Rising in interest still! Here you are introduced
to a new and most important personage—Lady Macbeth: her whose fiat is destiny to her feeble, fluctuating, and half-sinning husband. Here, that nothing may
be wanting, Shakespeare in the most artful, yet natural
manner, indirectly recapitulates the action of the third
scene, by Lady Macbeth reading part of a letter written

by her husband to her immediately after his interview
with the witches and with the messengers of Duncan :—

" They met me in the day of success: and I have learned by the per-
fectest report, they have more in them than mortal knowledge. When I
burned in desire to question them further, they made themselves air, into
which they vanished. Whiles I stood rapt in the wonder of it, came missives
from the King, who all-hailed me ' Thane of Cawdor ;' by which title, before,
these weird sisters saluted me, and referred me to the coming on of time, with
' Hail, King that shalt be !' This have I thought good to deliver thee, my
dearest partner of greatness ; that thou mightest not lose the dues of rejoicing,
by being ignorant of what greatness is promised thee. Lay it to thy heart,
and farewell."

Now comes a brief soliloquy, which artfully recalls to
recollection that of Macbeth in the preceding scene :—

" Glamis thou art, and Cawdor ; and shalt be
What thou art promised :—Yet do I fear thy nature ;
It is too full o' the milk of human kindness,
To catch the nearest way : thou wouldst be great ;
Art not without ambition ; but without
The illness should attend it. What thou wouldst highly,
That wouldst thou holily ; wouldst not play false,
And yet wouldst wrongly win : thou'dst have, great Glamis,
That which cries, 'Thus thou must do, if thou have it;
And that which rather thou dost fear to do,
Thou wishest should be undone.' Hie thee hither,
That I may pour my spirits in thine ear ;
And chastise with the valour of my tongue
All that impedes thee from the golden round,
Which fate and metaphysical aid doth seem
To have thee crowned withal."

Everywhere in Shakespeare you meet with this perfect
preserving of individuality in his characters. In their

sentiments, their passions, their actions, their reports of others, they are the same. Does not this soliloquy, especially the conclusion of it, remind you of the King's promise to visit Macbeth's castle? You know from the letter that Lady Macbeth has not the least anticipation of an occurrence so favourable to her guilty wishes. Are you not on the alert for the arrival of Macbeth with the news? How will she receive it? Shall he enter at once with it? Ha! that would be confounding things, jumbling high matters, such as the meeting, the welcome, the news, the consequence. The news must stand by itself, or it is good for nothing. A servant shall bring it,—not directly though, but by second hand. The actual bearer is almost dead with speed—has no more breath than would make up his errand at the gate—matter corroborative of the truth of the news. Here Lady Macbeth thoroughly opens her heart to you, thereby adding tenfold interest to the expected arrival of Macbeth. He arrives; and the contrast between the husband and the wife completes this inimitable scene, and leaves us all astir with horrible conjecture.

Another scene! Yes, and the climax rising still. You are not sure that the King will fulfil his promise of visiting Macbeth till he is actually at the gate of the castle. You must see him then; you must contemplate in her complete character the extraordinary woman to whom you have just been introduced. You must see

her lesson to Macbeth practised to perfection by the
teacher—

> "Look like the innocent flower,
> But be the serpent under it."

There is indeed the serpent under the flower; hidden!
not a warning scale to be seen, covered thoroughly and
thickly and impenetrably by the most winning blandish-
ments of duty and grace and sweetness! You could
scarcely believe that the tongue which speaks so blandly
its welcome to the King, could arm her husband's hand
with a dagger for the King's heart.

Scene the seventh. What! another scene yet? Yes!
And still the climax ascending? Yes! The master-scene
of the action. The victim of ambition is yet free from
guilt. His thought of heaven, his dread of retribution,
his respect for the claims of consanguinity, for the rights
of hospitality, his sense of the virtues of the King, keep
for a space aloof the demon whose fangs are on the watch
for him. Lady Macbeth enters, perceives his plight,
taunts him, reproaches him, threatens him, works upon
his false pride, shames him with the boast of what she
herself would do, and confirms him in the bloody purpose
which but a minute before he had half abandoned. The
murder of Duncan is fully, irrevocably resolved upon
and arranged, and you are brought to the close of an
act which is in itself a play,—unrivalled, unapproached
in modern or ancient times, perfect in symmetry and

dignity and vigour, with respect to which I defy human ingenuity to suggest addition or amendment or subtraction in any material point. I have been familiar with this play for upwards of forty years, and it is only now that its beauties are beginning to open upon me—now that I am attempting to analyze it. I have a feeling that were I permitted to live forty years more, and to attempt the same thing again, I should blush for my present work, so short, I fear, does it come of this almost superhuman creation. We are now prepared thoroughly for the second act.

Midnight; the deed is to be done. Blood! Shall it be set about at once? Not with the concurrence of Shakespeare. Where there is interest, there is generally a charm in gradual progression. Were the whole firmament to darken, to flame, and go out again in the transit of a moment, we should not be a thousandth part so much affected as by a single flash in any one quarter, from a crisis towards which we have watched the elements gradually approximating. The railroad abridges the royal pageant of half the impressiveness that is possessed upon the ordinary highway. How the funeral of Nelson swallowed up the soul in solemn, deep absorption as the procession marched, inch by inch as it were, up the Strand on its progress to St. Paul's. Speed, when not in itself the object of interest, contracts and impairs the impression of the senses. The long, fluctuating, rumbling roll of the thunder, communicates to us the full conception of sublimity; but a single clap, howsoever sudden and loud, affects us little more than the close report of a piece of ordnance, or even a fowling piece discharged unexpectedly. Few would count the days till the arrival of some great eclipse of the sun or the moon, were the eclipse to occupy only a few minutes of time, whereas millions now welcome the phenomenon. How impressively deepening is the one continuous interest from the first infringement of the disc till the engulphing of the orb in total obscuration, and thence to the emerging, the going through, and the thorough extrication of light from darkness. Shakespeare always takes care that *he* is not to blame if you forget the stages of his action. If you lose a link in the chain of his incidents and situations, this fault shall be your own. There is the hall of Macbeth's castle. It is pitch dark. You need not be reminded of the scene that closed the last act, and vowed the hand of Macbeth to the dagger, at the thought of which it shook at setting out. The flare of a torch approaches. It is Macbeth! No, it is Banquo! Banquo enters and speaks, and to the purpose. But not only is it with an indefinite prophetic feeling of the storm that is to come, that the mind of Banquo is labouring; the effects of the one that has

passed are not yet subsided. His reflections not only refer
you to what has passed, but are in keeping with all that
is to come, as the first bar of a dirge is in tone with those
that are to follow.   The after-swell of storm will at times
hold on till you wonder and question whence it comes, and
cannot guess, though it comes from the storm.   So the
effect of something that agitates violently the spirits will
continue, till you note it without connecting it with the
cause that produced it.   The impression which the interview with the witches has produced upon Banquo may be
clearly inferred from his comment, when the fulfilment of
the second prophetic " All hail!" is announced to Rosse
and Angus.

> "What!   Can the devil speak true?"

Coupling with that impression his emotions at the prophecies of the witches regarding himself, you cannot wonder
if his soul, agitated from its most secret depths, still
labours with the convulsion that has so disturbed it,
without his connecting the storm with the swell.   There
is something of the sublime in the obscure, unaccountable
depression of spirits under which Banquo tells us he is
labouring.   The flare of another torch.   It is Macbeth!
Yes.

> " I think not of them."

This is precisely in time with the remarks which Macbeth
addressed to Banquo on the heath in order to divert his

mind from the suspicion that he, Macbeth, attached any importance to the third prophetic salutation. But mark what follows. Mark the inconsistency, the instability of dissimulation :—

> " Yet, when we can entreat an hour to serve,
> Would spend it in some words upon that business,
> If you would grant the time."

He has thought of them, and betrays it the very moment after he has denied it. What is the meaning of this? A sudden thought of precaution that when the murder is discovered—as of course it must be, this mention of a consultation with reference to the third prophetic " All hail,"—the promise of royal haying—this hint of some enterprise to be attempted with a view to the fulfilment of that promise (for it is nothing else but a hint to that effect) may help to keep him clear from suspicion on the part of Banquo that he has had any hand in letting out the blood that is destined to flow that very night. Banquo's reply clearly establishes the fact :—

> " So I keep
> My bosom franchised, and allegiance clear,
> I shall be counselled."

It is a matter that may involve the question of honour and loyalty. Banquo retires. Now for the deed! Not yet; there is an attendant to be dismissed.

G

"Go, bid thy mistress, when my drink is ready,
She strike upon the bell.   Get thee to bed."

He is gone.   Here is situation! The man who has made
up his mind to murder his sovereign, kinsman, and guest,
stands now alone in his castle-hall at midnight, when
every one else has retired to rest—every one, except the
spiriting accomplice who has arranged with him the signal
when all is ready, when every head save his and hers is
fast upon its pillow, and he is at liberty to set about
the deed.   How do we feel?   Why we feel that were we
not aware of the dagger aerial that is about to invite the
hand of Macbeth, we should start as much as he does
when he sees it.

"Is this a dagger, which I see before me,
The handle toward my hand?   Come, let me clutch thee:—
I have thee not, and yet I see thee still.
Art thou not, fatal vision, sensible
To feeling, as to sight? or art thou but
A dagger of the mind; a false creation,
Proceeding from the heat-oppressèd brain?
I see thee yet, in form as palpable
As this which now I draw.
Thou marshal'st me the way that I was going;
And such an instrument I was to use.
Mine eyes are made the fools o' the other senses,
Or else worth all the rest: I see thee still:
And on thy blade, and dudgeon, gouts of blood,
Which was not so before.   There's no such thing:
It is the bloody business, which informs
Thus to mine eyes.   Now o'er the one half world

Nature seems dead, and wicked dreams abuse
The curtained sleeper; now witchcraft celebrates
Pale Hecate's offerings; and withered murder,
Alarumed by his sentinel, the wolf,
Whose howl's his watch, thus with his stealthy pace,
With Tarquin's ravishing strides, towards his design
Moves like a ghost.   Thou sure and firm-set earth,
Hear not my steps, which way they walk, for fear
Thy very stones prate of my where-about,
And take the present horror from the time,
Which now suits with it.   Whiles I threat, he lives;
Words to the heat of deeds too cold breath gives.   [*A bell rings.*
I go, and it is done; the bell invites me.
Hear it not, Duncan; for it is a knell
That summons thee to heaven, or to hell."

I have long entertained the opinion that this dagger is
not, as Macbeth assumes it to be, simply

" A dagger of the mind. . . . . .
Proceeding from the heat-opprossëd brain ; "

but on the contrary, an apparition coming and vanishing,
as the witches themselves do, and that consequently it
ought to be actually presented, as indeed it used to be.
In my mind the whole thing is too circumstantial, bears
too much upon the action, to justify the common interpretation which coincides with that of Macbeth.   It is a
phantom raised by the witches to draw Macbeth on to his
conclusion.   It is the supernatural coadjutor of Lady
Macbeth, dumbly but irresistibly persuading him to the
deed.   He falters yet.   Yes! upon the very threshold of

guilt he is faltering. But the evil agency of which he is
the victim is at hand with the dagger, shows him the
instrument he was to use, presents it to him with its
handle towards him, inviting him to clutch it as he
attempts to do, marshals for him with it the way he was
to go; nor withdraws it then, but while he is yet in
doubt whether it is substance or shadow that he looks
upon, ends the debate by exhibiting it to him stained with
gouts of blood—

" Which was not so before."

Macbeth's interpretation of the vision is not to be taken as
the truth.   It is not

" The bloody business which informs
Thus to his eyes."

He enters the fatal portal still preserving the identity of
his character, courting the very horror which his infirmity
aggravates.   Scarcely has he crossed the threshold, when
Lady Macbeth stands in the hall.   Here is situation
again.   Macbeth about the murder ; Lady Macbeth on
the watch for the issue ! Let us see what Shakespeare
will make of this situation.

From what we have already seen of Lady Macbeth,
we can hardly wonder at anything she performs, in the
way of daring and guilty achievement; yet the question

may be asked us, " Is it within the scope of human
capability that, woman as she is, she should present
herself at all; far less to tower over her husband as she
does, at such a crisis as this? Shakespeare is always prepared for such cases. Possibility is not enough for him.
The thing must be probable also. He knows that in all
natural incidents, there are bounds to credibility, and
that when credibility stops, interest refuses to go on.
Say that Lady Macbeth has no business in this scene?—
the moment she enters she makes her ample, consistent
apology—

> " That which hath made them drunk, hath made me bold ;
> What hath quenched them, hath given me fire."

Howsoever coolly we plan a desperate thing, the execution
tries us—ay, though our nerves be iron! She feels this
when the hour of action is at hand, and she fortifies herself
by the means whereby she disguises the drugs that chain
the grooms of the King to their couches; and whatsoever
obscure promptings she may experience of mistrust or fear,
she easily and thoroughly drowns—for what? That she
may go and see if all is prepared for the deed—if the King
sleeps—if the drugs have taken effect upon the grooms—
if it is safe to steal the daggers from their sheaths and lay
them ready. Don't wonder at her coming into the hall.
She has already been in the chamber that is about to flow
with blood. She hears a shriek,—

"Hark! Peace!
It was the owl that shrieked, the fatal bellman
That gives the stern'st good-night.—He is about it.
The doors are open; and the surfeited grooms
Do mock their charge with snores: I have drugged their possets,
That death and nature do contend about them,
Whether they live, or die.
    Macb. Who's there? What, ho!
    Lady Macb. Alack! I am afraid, they have awaked,
And 'tis not done:—the attempt, and not the deed,
Confounds us. Hark!—I laid their daggers ready:
He could not miss them.—Had he not resembled
My father as he slept, I had done it."

She has been at the bedside of the King with the
daggers of the grooms, and she would then and there
have anticipated Macbeth, and done the deed herself, had
not the King's resemblance to her father arrested her.
Some critics are fond of giving Lady Macbeth a great deal
of credit for this incident; but what is the real nature of
her compunction? What does the filial principle induce
her to abstain from? A gratuitous act of murder, an
act which she knows her husband is certain to perform
ere the flight of a quarter of an hour. How she must
thirst for the blood of the King! Where had been the
dagger had she entertained a doubt about the matter?
In the King's heart, as sure as she held it in her hand.
For my part, what would shake me more would be,
not that she abstained from the murder, but that under
the existing circumstances she ever thought of per-

✕ Without giving Lady Macbeth any credit for it, we may suppose these touches of remorse are produced to make us feel that she is a woman still and not a monster.

petrating it herself. You may depend upon it that Shakespeare never introduced this incident with the view of mitigating our abhorrence of his heroine. A great stress is sometimes laid upon the passage,—

> " I have given suck ; and know
> How tender 'tis to love the babe that milks me,"

as presenting a redeeming trait in Lady Macbeth's character. But we have only her own assertion ; and granting it to be true, what value do we attach to Lady Macbeth's notion of tenderness? Is it the tenderness of which a humane and gentle and truly feminine mother is susceptible? May we not assume, too, that she colours the circumstance with the view of shaming her husband into guilty resolution, by telling him how in defiance of nature's most holy law, *she* would have cleaved to her oath? She would have dashed out her infant's brains had she so sworn to it as Macbeth had sworn to murder Duncan! And yet she knows how tender 'tis to love the babe that milks her. I think we may infer, from the nature of her boast, the tenderness of her maternal feelings. I form my idea of Lady Macbeth's character, not from what she says, but from what she does.

Macbeth enters. She exclaims immediately upon seeing him, " My husband!" This is very fine. This is

truth of feeling on the part of Shakespeare—subtle perception of the workings of the heart.　She quails for
a moment, she fears Macbeth has miscarried in the
attempt which perhaps he had never made except for
her.　We have never heard her call him anything before but Glamis, Cawdor, Thane.　What is the term
which the thought of utter ruin now suggests to her?
That which is a pledge for protection and cleaving—
" My husband!"

> " *Macb.* I have done the deed."

All's right, and she is herself again, collected, firm.　The
dialogue here is epigrammatic and almost monosyllabic;
but every word teems with import.

> "Didst thou not hear a noise?
> *Lady Macb.* I heard the owl scream, and the crickets cry;
> Did not you speak?
> *Macb.*　　　　When?
> *Lady Macb.*　　　　　Now!
> *Macb.*　　　　　　　　As I descended?
> *Lady Macb.* Ay!
> *Macb.* Hark!"

Here is situation.　Who breathes?　It is a false alarm.
Some actors, to make manifest to the audience the
horror and terror of Macbeth during this critical pause,
bring their hands together so as to cause the blades to
vibrate audibly against one another.　Here is the danger
of studying partial effects.　This was forestalling Shake-

speare. This was attracting Lady Macbeth's attention to
the daggers before the time. Would she not have heard
them? As sure as she was Lady Macbeth. Macbeth re-
covering from his momentary alarm, continues:—

> " Who lies in the second chamber ?
>   *Lady Macb.*   Donalbain.
>   *Macb.* This is a sorry sight !
>   *Lady Macb.* A foolish thought to say a sorry sight.
>   *Macb.* There's one did laugh in his sleep, and one cried ' Murder !'
> That they did wake each other ; I stood and heard them :
> But they did say their prayers, and addressed them
> Again to sleep.
>   *Lady Macb.* There are two lodged together.
>   *Macb.* One cried ' God bless us !' and, ' Amen,' the other ;
> As they had seen me with these hangman's hands.
> Listening their fear, I could not say, ' Amen,'
> When they did say, ' God bless us ! '
>   *Lady Macb.*   Consider it not so deeply—
>   *Macb.* But wherefore could not I pronounce ' Amen ? '
> I had most need of blessing, and ' Amen '
> Stuck in my throat."

This is the shock of guilt. This is the collapse of the
soul. The moment crime is perpetrated, the mind is
shaken in its propriety, and the tongue utters what is
uppermost without regard to relevancy or reason.

> " *Lady Macb.*   These deeds must not be thought
> After these ways ; so, it will make us mad."

Here on her part begins the gnawing of the mental cancer
that in the fourth act heaves her, sleeping, from her

pillow to walk the chamber in a dream. Here she half suspects the impossibility of silencing the importunate remembrancer—conscience.

> "*Macb.* Methought, I heard a voice cry, ' Sleep no more !
> Macbeth does murder sleep, the innocent sleep ;
> Sleep, that knits up the ravelled sleave of care,
> The death of each day's life, sore labour's bath,
> Balm of hurt minds, great nature's second course,
> Chief nourisher in life's feast.' "

This rushing crowd of figures is all truth. Passion is the mistress of imagination, and ever, when highly excited, brings imagination into play. He now fully appreciates the murder which he has committed upon his own peace, while its consequences rise up like so many phantoms, and rapidly arrange themselves before him. The sleep, the rich blessing of which perhaps he had never thought of before, now looking back upon him as it bids him an eternal farewell, points, as it were, to all the modes in which it ministers to the refreshment, the solace, the beguilement, the comfort, the enjoyment of those to whom its heavenly visitations are permitted.

> "*Lady Macb.* What do you mean ?"

He continues :—

> "Still it cried, ' Sleep no more !' to all the house."

How loud is the cry of conscience in the guilty!

> " Glamis hath murdered sleep, and therefore Cawdor
> Shall sleep no more : Macbeth shall sleep no more !"

Here is a hint to conscience. Examine the effect which
this scene produces upon yourselves, and from your own
impression calculate how its effect may tell upon the
mind that feels a temptation to break within " the bloody
house of life ; " and then debate whether there is utter
rashness in asserting that this scene has been instrumental
in preventing the commission of murder. And if it has
not, it is hard to conceive how any homily or sermon has
ever been attended with that result. And if you demand
a corroborative argument in support of that assertion, I
give you what I conceive to be next to the absolute
establishment of the fact, the most conclusive one—in the
dead stillness of a whole theatre of living human beings
converted for the time into statues by the petrifying
horror of this scene !

> " *Lady Macb.* Who was it that thus cried ? Why, worthy Thane,
> You do unbend your noble strength, to think
> So brainsickly of things :—Go, get some water,
> And wash this filthy witness from your hand."

And now for the first time she sees the daggers.

> " Why did you bring these daggers from the place ? "

Here Macbeth's inaptness for the deed betrays itself
again. In the preceding scene he himself had suggested,
that to throw suspicion upon the grooms, their daggers

should be used. In his confusion he forgets his own act of forethought. He has brought the daggers away. He is unconscious that he still retains them. He looks at his hands, but he sees nothing except the blood. The stain of his soul is everywhere within him and without him and all around him. He is incapable of being cognizant of anything else!

> " Why did you bring these daggers from the place ?
> They must lie there.   Go carry them ; and smear
> The sleepy grooms with blood."

The commands of her of whose reproaches, scoffs, and threats he has hitherto been the slave, are virtueless here. No! the whole world could not tempt him or compel him to go back.

> " *Macb.*   I'll go no more :
> I am afraid to think what I have done ;
> Look on't again, I dare not."

Hear Lady Macbeth. Hear the woman that knows how tender 'tis to love the babe that milks her; that is dissuaded from murdering with her own hand the sleeping King by the remembrance of her father :—

> " *Lady Macb.*   Infirm of purpose !
> Give me the daggers.   The sleeping, and the dead,
> Are but as pictures."

That is, they have as much perception.

> " 'Tis the eye of childhood,
> That fears a painted devil. If he do bleed,
> I'll gild the faces of the grooms withal,
> For it must seem their guilt."

It is singular that even Mrs. Siddons should have missed the true import of these lines, which are quite superfluous and impertinent except as a taunt at Macbeth, reminding him of his own arrangement, and the imbecility that prevents him from carrying it into execution.

> " Will it not be received,
> When we have marked with blood those sleepy two
> Of his own chamber, and used their very daggers,
> That they have done 't ? "

She enters the chamber and Macbeth is left horribly alone, all sense and consciousness swallowed up in the perdition of the deed which he has committed. He stands chained to the spot by guilt; and the audience sit chained as fast to their seats. What shall astound him now as not the loudest clap of thunder could? A knock at the castle-gate. The thought of a single human eye has now more terror in it than the glaring of a thousand lightnings. What does he think of now? The blood upon his hands.

> " *Macb.*   Whence is that knocking?
> How is't with me, when every noise appals me?
> What hands are here! Ha! they pluck out mine eyes !
> Will all great Neptune's ocean wash this blood

Clean from my hand ?   No ; this my hand will rather
The multitudinous seas incarnardine,
Making the green—one red !"

Here Lady Macbeth enters, fortunately for herself and
her husband.   He is now incapable of thought, volition,
or action.   He could not stir though the roof were falling
upon him,—or worse,—though the gate were opening,
and the visitors just about to enter.

"*Lady Macb.* My hands are of your colour ; but I shame
To wear a heart so white."

The knocking is repeated :—

"I hear a knocking
At the south entry :—retire we to our chamber :
A little water clears us of this deed :
How easy is it then !   Your constancy
Hath left you unattended.—[*Knocking again.*]   Hark ! more knocking :
Get on your night-gown, lest occasion call us,
And show us to be watchers :—be not lost
So poorly in your thoughts."

She reasons with him, she counsels him, she reproves him,
she grasps him by the arm and shakes him.   She looks
for consciousness in a block of marble.   As the knocking
is more and more repeated, she grows more and more
desperate, and at last endeavours by main force to drag
him from the precipice on the brink of which he stands,
fascinated by the very danger which threatens him with
toppling over.   The last violent appeal is successful.

" *Macb.* To know my deed,—'twere best not know myself."
[*Knocking again.*]

What does he in his now desperation? He calls frantic-
ally to the unwelcome, untimely summons—

" Wake, Duncan, with thy knocking! Ay, would, thou couldst!"

Here the porter enters, and to gain time there is given a
soliloquy which is now judiciously omitted, and for the
nature of portions of which we must blame Shakespeare's
times and not him; though it is perfectly consistent with
the temperament of a low fellow, who, participating in
the general festivity in honour of the royal visit, has been
carousing till the second cock, and is summoned from his
bed half rested and recruited. The gate is opened, and
Macduff and Lenox enter.

" Goes the King hence to-day?"

The actor who betrays to the audience in any portion of
this scene the slightest evidence of desperation or forget-
fulness on the part of Macbeth, errs most egregiously
from true judgment. The audience require no hint as
to what is passing in Macbeth's bosom, nor is there a
moment's opportunity for by-play, as it is called, to render the thing feasible. He is kept in close conversation
from first to last. If he is on his guard with respect

to one of the visitors, be sure he is equally so with respect to both. How absurd is it, then, for an actor to require that this question shall be repeated, as if, absorbed in his expectation of what is coming, Macbeth did not hear it in the first instance. Macbeth's mind being once aroused to the necessity of playing his part, the imminency of his danger keeps it broad awake. He would as soon betray himself to Lenox by standing gasping after Macduff, as he would betray himself to Macduff by being abstracted when the Thane inquires if the King is stirring yet? When the discovery of the murder came, would not Lenox recollect the statue he had spoken to, and guess the cause which had turned Macbeth for the time into a stone? The frame of mind in which we now find Macbeth would rather induce him to overdo than to fall short. Here is again the mischief of studying partial effects. Howsoever calm Macbeth may appear without, the storm shall not only be kept up within, but with aggravated strife. Here again is situation, and powerful situation too. Macbeth obliged to listen, while Lenox recounts the horrors of the night; he himself all the while expecting every moment to hear the voice and footsteps of Macduff, as the Thane rushes, which he is sure to do, in amazement and trepidation and horror, from the chamber of blood. He comes.

> " *Macd.* O, horror ! horror ! horror ! Tongue, nor heart,
> .   Cannot conceive, nor name thee !

Macb. }
Len. }   What's the matter?

Macd. Confusion now hath made his masterpiece!
Most sacrilegious murder hath broke ope
The Lord's anointed temple, and stole thence
The life o' the building.

    Macb.   What is't you say? the life?

    Len. Mean you his majesty?

    Macd. Approach the chamber, and destroy your sight
With a new Gorgon :—Do not bid me speak ;
See, and then speak yourselves.   [*Exeunt* MACBETH *and* LENOX.
                         Awake! awake!
Ring the alarum bell :—Murder! and treason!
Banquo, and Donalbain! Malcolm! awake!
Shake off this downy sleep, death's counterfeit;
And look on death itself! up, up and see
The great doom's image!—Malcolm! Banquo!
As from your graves rise up, and walk like sprights,
To countenance this horror!   [*Bell rings.*

And now let us inquire how the presence of Lady Macbeth can be dispensed with at this juncture. Would she take a share in every other scene of the tragic enterprise, and absent herself from this last and most critical one? She who in a former scene, when Macbeth asks her—

           " Will it not be received,
When we have marked with blood those sleepy two
Of his own chamber, and used their very daggers,
That they have done 't ? "

She who when thus interrogated replies—

           " Who dares receive it other,
As we shall make our grief and clamour roar
Upon his death ? "

I

would she not put into practice what she herself had pre-
concerted? Is the scene complete without her? Is it fit
that the master spirit should be away when its agency is
most needed? Is Lady Macbeth aware of the unstable
nature of her husband? Has she proved and combated it
in every deal of the game, and now that the final, deciding
hand is to be played, and the game lost or won, will she
not be by with the stimulus and support of her presence
to keep his constancy at the sticking-place to which she
has again screwed it; when well she knows, from repeated
experience, that her presence will supply the place of
manhood in him, should he falter, or waver, or harbour a
thought of quailing? Will she absent herself when she is
most wanted? When the result of her absence may be
utter, irretrievable, disgraceful, and damning ruin? Does
she recollect the state in which she has just dragged
Macbeth from the hall, from the imminent danger of de-
tection, into the privity, secrecy, and security of his
chamber; and does she desert him there? As the mistress
of the castle, why should she keep her room when the
alarm bell is tempestuously swinging, while her stairs and
corridors are thronged with the rush of feet in amazeful
haste, and reverberate with the outcry of wailing and
consternation? Would it not be suspicious that, while
the whole castle is afoot, the mistress of it should remain
sitting? There is every reason for Lady Macbeth's co-
operation in this scene, and not one for her absence,

except the reason of the actress who personates Lady Macbeth, that it is not worth while to come on for three or four times for the mere sake of probability and propriety; or the reason of an actor or stage-manager who thinks that it is best "to come to Hecuba," though he should overturn common-sense and nature in his speed. Our stage has been injured, and the taste of our audiences vitiated by the studying of mere effect. Shakespeare perfectly well knew where Lady Macbeth or any other woman would be found at such a juncture. Not in her bed-chamber, or in her dressing-chamber, or in her sitting-chamber, but in her hall, in the very midst of the hurly-burly. And there he has placed her, to suffer the rebuke of the actor, to be told most ignorantly that she has no business there, and to be sent to her chamber again, where if even on account of her mere anxiety as to the issue, she could not have remained; though the door had been locked upon her, she would have broken it open, and rushed forth and played her part in the universal din.

> " *Enter* LADY MACBETH.
> What's the business,
> That such a hideous trumpet calls to parley
> The sleepers of the house! speak, speak.—
>   *Macd.*   O, gentle lady,
> 'Tis not for you to hear what I can speak:
> The repetition, in a woman's ear
> Would murder as it fell.
>   *Enter* BANQUO.
>   O Banquo, Banquo,

Our royal master's murdered!
   Lady Macb.   Woe, alas!
What, in our house?
   Ban.   Too cruel, anywhere—
Dear Duff, I prithee, contradict thyself,
And say, it is not so.

       Re-enter MACBETH *and* LENOX.

   Macb. Had I but died an hour before this chance
I had lived a blessed time; for, from this instant,
There's nothing serious in mortality:
All is but toys: renown, and grace, is dead;
The wine of life is drawn, and the mere lees
Is left this vault to brag of.

       Enter MALCOLM *and* DONALBAIN.

   Don. What is amiss?
   Macb.   You are, and do not know it:
The spring, the head, the fountain of your blood
Is stopped: the very source of it is stopped.
   Macd. Your royal father's murdered.
   Mal.   O, by whom?
   Len. Those of his chamber, as it seemed, had done 't,
Their hands and faces were all badged with blood,
So were their daggers, which, unwiped, we found
Upon their pillows:
They stared, and were distracted: no man's life
Was to be trusted with them.
   Macb. O, yet I do repent me of my fury,
That I did kill them.
   Macd.   Wherefore did you so? "

Here is the danger. Here is the point of salvation or
ruin. Here is the chance—the scaffold or the throne!
Here occurs the strongest reason for the presence of
Lady Macbeth. Macduff makes no attempt to conceal
that he attaches suspicion to the fact of Macbeth's having

slain the grooms. Macbeth must extricate himself here thoroughly and at once by vindicating what appears questionable. It is brink-work here for both the husband and the wife. Take the latter away, the situation is deprived of half its impressiveness. And who doubts that he is not only heartened, but inspired by her presence? He gasps while he replies :—

> " Who can be wise, amazed, temperate, and furious,
> Loyal, and neutral, in a moment ? No man :
> The expedition of my violent love
> Outran the pauser, reason.—Here lay Duncan,
> His silver skin laced with his golden blood ;
> And his gashed stabs looked like a breach in nature,
> For ruin's wasteful entrance : there, the murderers,
> Steeped in the colours of their trade, their daggers
> Unmannerly breeched with gore : who could refrain,
> That had a heart to love, and in that heart
> Courage, to make his love known ? "

The danger is warded off for the time. By this last act of boldness and self-collectedness, he atones for all past remissness and weakness and vacillation. Her spirit is reassured. Her presence is now no longer necessary. She affects natural exhaustion, in which she is in no small degree aided by that sudden revulsion of the spirits which attends the transition from the extreme of danger to escape and comparative security, and she cries to be assisted out. After another short scene descriptive of the effect of Duncan's murder on the visitors at Macbeth's castle, the act terminates.

And now that we have gone over this act, and dealt and expatiated upon every important portion of it, allow me to ask if there is instruction in it or not, if it is a lesson or idleness, if the effect is serviceable or injurious? In one word, does it denounce or recommend the perpetration of crime? I shall not wrong your judgment by supposing that there can be any other answer but this one: it is a luminous exposition of the revolting, hideous nature of guilt, and of the agony and degradation which it entails. Contemplate Macbeth in this act, and recall the image of the man who in the third scene of the first act presented himself to you, flushed with the honest pride of victory achieved in a virtuous cause. What is he now? A livid, nerveless, quaking coward, whose eyes are plucked out, as it were, by the sight of that with which the havoc of a hundred fields has made them familiar and perfectly at home. Or contemplate Lady Macbeth, playing the hypocrite, palming off the after lie, in her simulated ignorance of the cause of the universal, hideous uproar; her well-acted horror at the announcement of that cause, and the assumed exhaustion which bears her triumphant from the scene, the moment she has played her part; and contrast with her here, the woman whose towering spirit, though displaying itself in a reprehensible cause, shortly before excited your astonishment —almost your admiration.

PART THE THIRD.

NO man, except a scholar well versed in the drama, should ever be allowed to assume the acting management of a theatre. The individual who undertakes such a charge should be especially a man of mind. How powerfully was this exemplified in the instance of the late John Philip Kemble. What a reformation did he effect in the stage. Before his time, the scenic picture was composed of parts incongruous. Tailors and mantua-makers seem to have been regarded as a race unknown to antiquity. Rome in the days of Cæsar, as represented on the stage, stared upon the costume of London, perambulating her classic streets, in all the cumbersome, ungainly formality of attire which prevailed in the reign of the first Georges. The disappearance of this barbarous anomaly was the result of entrusting the acting management to the hands of Mr. Kemble. This recalls to me a conversation which

I once had with Mr. Macready, in the course of which we discussed the manner of representing the witches in the play of "Macbeth." I was particularly struck with an alteration which he suggested, with reference to the business of the incantation scene, and which I thought reflected the highest credit upon his taste and acuteness as a critic, an alteration which he has now effected, and in proposing which he was perfectly borne out by the action and the text.

The effect of any momentous occurrence depends on many things besides its own intrinsic importance. The preparation for any spectacle, whether the triumphant entry of a conqueror or the ignominious exit of a criminal, tells upon our interest almost as powerfully as the spectacle itself. In the ordinary way of managing the opening of this scene, the idea that the witches expect Hecate, that they wait her approach with the feverish restlessness of malign spirits, keen in the prosecution of their forbidden work, is never conveyed to the audience. Upon the rising of the curtain the witches are discovered, standing round the cauldron, and the dialogue begins without any preparatory business, which, by making the reference of the introductory lines clear and striking, would communicate to them all the effect which they are capable of receiving. Imagine the dark and dreary cavern; the work, to the consummating of which it is appropriated; the unearthly and accursed beings who

superintend that work. What a picture should it suggest!
Let the witches be placed in different parts of the cavern.
Suppose one at the mouth, intently on the watch; another
near the cauldron, cowering over the livid flame,—which
by the way should be placed under the charmed pot and
not in it; the third witch on the side opposite the entrance, seated perhaps upon a fragment of stone, her arms
folded, and rocking to and fro, upon the rack as it were
of impatience. Let not a word be spoken, till the audience
have had time to study the picture. 'Tis to the point,
and they are sure to feel it, if you will allow them. The
brinded cat, the hedge-pig, and Harper, are of course the
familiars of the witches, and are supposed to be stationed
without the cavern to give notice of the approach of Hecate. The first witch hears her familiar:—

" Thrice the brinded cat hath mewed."

The eyes of the other witches are instantly turned towards
her: a pause ensues during which they all remain motion-
less. The witch near the cauldron hears her familiar;
she starts from her cowering attitude:—

" Thrice; and once the hedge-pig whined."

Another pause here. Now at length the third witch
springs upon her feet:—"Harper cries;" and then ad-
dressing her sisters, and not putting words into Harper's

mouth, which Shakespeare never intended for him:—
"'Tis time, 'tis time."

Since I have directed your attention to this scene, I
shall venture, if you will allow me, to present you with a
reading of it by Edmund Kean, whose views as to the
personation of the witches exactly correspond with those
of Macready.

ACT IV.

Scene I.—*A cavern. In the middle a boiling cauldron.
Thunder. Enter the three Witches.*

" *1st Witch.* Thrice the brinded cat hath mewed.
2nd Witch. Thrice ; and once the hedge-pig whined.
3rd Witch. Harper cries.——'Tis time, 'tis time.
1st Witch. Round about the cauldron go ;
In the poisoned entrails throw.—
Toad, that under coldest stone
Days and nights hath thirty-one
Sweltered venom, sleeping got,
Boil thou first in the charmèd pot !
All. Double, double toil and trouble ;
Fire, burn ; and, cauldron, bubble.
2nd Witch. Fillet of a fenny snake,
In the cauldron boil and bake ;
Eye of newt and toe of frog,
Wool of bat and tongue of dog,
Adder's fork and blind-worm's sting,
Lizard's leg and owlet's wing,
For a charm of powerful trouble,
Like a hell-broth boil and bubble.
All. Double, double toil and trouble ;
Fire, burn ; and, cauldron, bubble.
3rd Witch. Scale of dragon, tooth of wolf,
Witch's mummy ; maw and gulf

Of the ravined salt-sea shark ;
Root of hemlock, digged i' the dark ;
Liver of blaspheming Jew ;
Gall of goat ; and slips of yew,
Slivered in the moon's eclipse ;
Nose of Turk, and Tartar's lips ;
Finger of birth-strangled babe,
Ditch-delivered by a drab ;
Make the gruel thick and slab :
Add thereto a tiger's chaudron,
For the ingredients of our cauldron.
   All. Double, double toil and trouble ;
Fire, burn ; and, cauldron, bubble.
   2nd Witch. Cool it with a baboon's blood ;
Then the charm is firm and good.

Enter HECATE *and the other three Witches.*

   Hec. O, well done ! I commend your pains ;
And every one shall share i' the gains :
And now about the cauldron sing,
Like elves and fairies in a ring,
Enchanting all that you put in.

   [*Music and a song, " Black Spirits," &c.* HECATE *retires.*

   2nd Witch. By the pricking of my thumbs,
Something wicked this way comes.—
      Open, locks,
      Whoever knocks !

Enter MACBETH.

   Macb. How now, you secret, black, and midnight hags !
What is't you do ?
   All.   A deed without a name.
   Macb. I conjure you, by that which you profess,
Howe'er you come to know it, answer me :
Though you untie the winds and let them fight
Against the churches ; though the yesty waves
Confound and swallow navigation up ;
Though bladed corn be lodg'd, and trees blown down ;

Though castles topple on their warders' heads ;
Though palaces and pyramids do slope
Their heads to their foundations ; though the treasure
Of nature's germins tumble all together,
Even till destruction sicken ; answer me
To what I ask you.

 1st Witch. Speak.

 2nd Witch.   Demand.

 3rd Witch.   We'll answer.

 1st Witch. Say, if thou'dst rather hear it from our mouths,
Or from our masters' ?

 Macb. Call 'em ; let me see 'em.

 1st Witch. Pour in sow's blood, that hath eaten
Her nine farrow ; grease that's sweaten
From the murderer's gibbet, throw
Into the flame.

 All. Come, high, or low ;
Thyself and office deftly show !

   Thunder First Apparition : an armed Head arises.

 Macb. Tell me, thou unknown power,—

 1st Witch. He knows thy thought :
Hear his speech, but say thou nought.

 1st App. Macbeth ! Macbeth ! Macbeth ! Beware Macduff !
Beware the thane of Fife.—Dismiss me.—Enough. [*Descends.*

 Macb. Whate'er thou art, for thy good caution, thanks.
Thou hast harped my fear aright ; but one word more :—

 1st Witch. He will not be commanded : here's another,
More potent than the first.

   Thunder. Second Apparition : a bloody Child.

 2nd App. Macbeth ! Macbeth ! Macbeth !

 Macb. Had I three ears, I'd hear thee.

 2nd App. Be bloody, bold, and resolute ; laugh to scorn
The power of man ; for none of woman born
Shall harm Macbeth.   [*Descends.*

 Macb. Then live Macduff : what need I fear of thee ?
But yet I'll make assurance doubly sure,

And take a bond of fate: thou shalt not live:
That I may tell pale-hearted fear it lies,
And sleep in spite of thunder.

Thunder. Third Apparition: a Child crowned, with a tree in his hand.

           What is this
That rises like the issue of a king,
And wears upon his baby brow the round
And top of sovereignty?
  All.   Listen, but speak not to 't.
 3rd App. Be lion-mettled, proud; and take no care
Who chafes, who frets, or where conspirers are;
Macbeth shall never vanquished be, until
Great Birnam wood to high Dunsinane hill
Shall come against him.   [*Descends.*
  Macb.   That will never be:
Who can impress the forest, bid the tree
Unfix his earth-bound root? Sweet bodements, good!
Rebellious head, rise never, till the wood
Of Birnam rise, and our high-placed Macbeth
Shall live the lease of nature, pay his breath
To time and mortal custom.—Yet my heart
Throbs to know one thing: tell me, if your art
Can tell so much, shall Banquo's issue ever
Reign in this kingdom?
  All.   Seek to know no more.
  Macb. I will be satisfied: deny me this
And an eternal curse fall on you! Let me know:—
Why sinks that cauldron? and what noise is this?   [*Hautboys.*
 1st Witch. Show!
 2nd Witch. Show!
 3rd Witch. Show!
 All. Show his eyes, and grieve his heart;
Come like shadows, so depart!

    [*A show of eight kings, the last with a glass in his hand;*
        Banquo's ghost following.

  Macb. Thou art too like the spirit of Banquo: down!
Thy crown does sear mine eye-balls. And thy hair,

Thou other gold-bound brow, is like the first :—
A third is like the former.—Filthy hags !
Why do you show me this?—A fourth ? start, eyes !
What, will the line stretch out to the crack of doom ?
Another yet ?—a seventh ! I'll see no more :—
And yet the eighth appears, who bears a glass,
Which shows me many more ; and some I see,
That two-fold balls and treble sceptres carry.
Horrible sight !—Now, I see, 'tis true ;
For the blood-boltered Banquo smiles upon me,
And points at them for his.—   [*Apparitions vanish.*
What, is this so ?

   1st Witch. Ay, sir, all this is so :—but why
Stands Macbeth thus amazedly ?
Come, sisters, cheer we up his sprights,
And show the best of our delights :
I'll charm the air to give a sound,
While you perform your antique round ;
That this great king may kindly say,
Our duties did his welcome pay.

   [*Music. The Witches dance, and then vanish with* HECATE.

   Macb. Where are they ? Gone ?—Let this pernicious hour
Stand aye accursëd in the calendar.—
Come in, without there !

Enter LENOX.

   Len. What's your grace's will ?
   Macb. Saw you the weird sisters ?
   Len.   No, my lord.
   Macb. Came they not by you ?
   Len.   No indeed, my lord.
   Macb. Infected be the air whereon they ride ;
And damned all those that trust them ! I did hear
The galloping of horse : who was't came by ?
   Len. 'Tis two or three, my lord, that bring you word
Macduff is fled to England.
   Macb.   Fled to England !
   Len. Ay, my good lord.

Macb. Time, thou anticipatest my dread exploits:
The flighty purpose never is o'ertook
Unless the deed go with it ; from this moment,
The very firstlings of my heart shall be
The firstlings of my hand.   And even now
To crown my thoughts with acts, be it thought and done :
The castle of Macduff I will surprise ;
Seize upon Fife ; give to the edge o' the sword
His wife, his babes, and all unfortunate souls
That trace him in his line.   No boasting like a fool,
This deed I'll do before this purpose cool.

PART THE FOURTH.

OW consummate is the skill which Shakespeare displays in keeping up the interest of " Macbeth," from the banquet scene to the catastrophe. Duncan is despatched. Banquo is despatched. The sons of the King and Macduff are fled to England. No one is left that we care much about who may become the victim to another deed of blood, and whose jeopardy preserves the tension of that horror which has been hitherto kept upon the strain. The manner in which the usurper is to end his career, is the only incident about which we are now solicitous; yet two whole acts remain to be gone through. Upon that incident alone did Shakespeare construct the last two acts of his tragedy. He proposes it in the very first scene of the fourth act, and keeps it constantly in view till the termination of the last scene of the fifth, without ever

wearying the patience of the audience in allowing their
expectation to flag. He involves it in constant doubt and
perplexity. Macbeth is threatened with his doom—he is
assured against it. It approaches him—he defies it. One
ground of confidence having vanished, he clings to the
other; that also fails him. He has nothing but his
despair to confide in; he trusts in it and falls!

At the close of the third act, he avows his determination to consult the weird sisters as to his destiny:—

> " I will to-morrow,
> (Betimes I will), to the weird sisters:
> More shall they speak ; for now I am bent to know,
> By the worst means, the worst."

In prosecution of this intention, he presents himself in the
Pit of Acheron. One apparition darkly announces his
fate:—

> " Macbeth ! Macbeth ! Macbeth !
> Beware Macduff !
> Beware the Thane of Fife."

Another partly dispels the fear which this warning had
confirmed:—

> " Macbeth ! Macbeth ! Macbeth !
> Be bloody, bold, and resolute ! Laugh to scorn
> The power of man, for none of woman born
> Shall harm Macbeth."

The third puts the seal as it were to the assurance:—

L

> " Be lion-mettled, proud ; and take no care
> Who chafes, who frets, or where conspirers are :
> Macbeth shall never vanquished be, until
> Great Birnam wood to high Dunsinane hill
> Shall come against him."

The first of these announcements has its effect in de-
noting the cause of the action. It prompts Macbeth to an
act which whets, as it were, the weapon by which he is
destined to fall. He resolves on the death of Macduff,
finds that he has fled to England, and in the fury of dis-
appointment puts his whole family to the sword. It also
enhances, in the peculiar argument for revenge with which
it supplies Macduff, the fury of the storm which is about
to burst upon the Usurper's head and blast him. His
Thanes desert him. He is regardless of it :—

> " Bring me no more reports ; let them fly all ;
> Till Birnam wood remove to Dunsinane,
> I cannot taint with fear. What's the boy Malcolm ?
> Was he not born of woman ? The spirits that know
> All mortal consequence, have pronounced me thus :
> ' Fear not, Macbeth ; no man, that's born of woman,
> Shall e'er have power on thee !' Then fly, false thanes,
> And mingle with the English epicures :
> The mind I sway by, and the heart I bear,
> Shall never sagg with doubt, nor shake with fear."

He hears of the approach of the English. It never appals
him :—

> " I'll fight till from my bones the flesh be hack'd."

And again :—

> " I will not be afraid of death and bane,
> Till Birnam forest come to Dunsinane ! "

At length, his confidence receives a check. The wood
is reported to be coming. All the foundation of his hopes
has given way. He apprehends the demolition of the
whole fabric, but still it stands—

> " For none of woman born shall harm Macbeth."

He sallies from his castle to meet the assailants in the
field. Armed with this prediction, he fearlessly commits
himself to the surge of battle; till, encountering Macduff,
he is, for a moment, appalled by the recollection of the
warning which counselled him to avoid his adversary, and
by the sense of guilt which renders intolerable the sight
of the man whom he has so grievously wronged. They
fight. Macduff makes no impression upon the tyrant.
Macbeth, forgetting everything in his exultation at the
belief that he is invulnerable, cannot refrain from vaunting
the charmed life with which he is endowed.

> " Thou losest labour :
> As easy mayst thou the intrenchant air
> With thy keen sword impress, as make me bleed :
> Let fall thy blade on vulnerable crests ;
> I wear a charmëd life, which must not yield
> To one of woman born ! "

How powerfully this situation must have told upon the

audience before whom " Macbeth " was first represented :
how every heart must have throbbed ;—since with us, who
almost have the play by heart, it never fails to produce an
effect perfectly absorbing.   Is there an individual who
does not hold his breath while he witnesses it? Who does
not sit like a statue?   Who is not all ears and eyes,
watching the regicide, as he towers like a pinnacle round
which a tempest plays, and which you expect every moment to be struck from its base by a thunderbolt? His
fate is at hand, it is suspended only by the breath of
Macduff.   It leaps upon him with the suddenness and
force of a flash of lightning, and blasts him where he
stands :—

> " Despair thy charm ;
> And let the angel, whom thou still hast served,
> Tell thee, Macduff was from his mother's womb
> Untimely ripped ! "

Here was the dramatist.   Here was perception of the use
of situation and incident.   And here let me recommend
the modern hypercritic to apply for such a lesson of ingen-
uousness, discretion, and justice as will prevent him from
denouncing the modern dramatist for availing himself of
the instruments which Shakespeare deemed it no disgrace
to use,—nay, from which there was never yet a popular
play that did not derive a considerable portion of its
effect.   The whole play of " Macbeth " is a chain of

incidents and situations; nor is this the least part of
its merit. Why should it be? What are incident and
situation? Are they not the great springs of human interest? Do they not supply us with the poetry of human
life? Are they not the things that make the canvas of the
artist breathe and glow, that warm and soften the marble
of the sculptor into flesh? What burst of poetry in
" Paradise Lost" can surpass the incident which, at the
close of Satan's narration of his triumph over the innocence of man, at the moment that he listens for the
applauding peal of millions of .Cherubim and Seraphim,
assails his ear with one universal hiss, and casts him from
his throne, a reptile crawling upon the floor of Pandemo-
nium? Incident and situation! They cause the stir of
life, upon the mimic or the real stage of which they rouse
us, set our feelings and imaginations to work, play with
our pulses, drive the blood from our cheeks or bring it
into them, distend our breasts with sighs, set the fountains
of our 'tears a-flowing, do with us what they list. They
are a power, and convict of the grossest obtuseness of
intellect and the most egregious swerving from ingenuous-
ness, the man who sets them down for imbecility. They
are the sinews not only of the dramatic but also of the
epic poet. The fine arts had never lived and stood without them. The genuineness of their dignity is attested
by the sign manual of Homer and Shakespeare and
Raphael; and let him be excommunicated from the

republic of letters, who condemns himself by despising them. One word and no more. "Macbeth" is the most melodramatic tragedy in the whole range of the drama, and it is to the credit of Shakespeare that it is so.

PART THE FIFTH.

NOT only is the observance of unities not essential, but absolutely hostile to the excellence of the drama. Had it been respected, where would have been the broad and bold delineation, the light and shade, the modulation, as it were, of character, as exemplified in the dramas of Shakespeare? What scope would there have been for the play of the pencil, that has so vividly, so convincingly, portrayed the birth and growth and perfection of the most powerful passions of our species? Where would have been the story of Macbeth? How magnificent and instructive a portrait should we have lost of guilty ambition in all its fearful stages—its portentous infancy, its appalling maturity, the gradual hardening of the usurper's heart from flesh to steel! The man—who at first recoils at the

idea of shedding the blood of the king that stood in his
way;—that feat achieved, gratuitously imbrues his hands
in the blood of his friend and companion-in-arms, and after
the consummation of that deed revels, as it were, in the
promiscuous slaughter of a whole family and race.   Then,
the heart-freezing spectacle of isolated guilt, with every
source of earthly aggrandisement at its command, cut off
on every side from sympathy, attachment, and alliance.

> " This supernatural soliciting
> Cannot be ill; cannot be good.   If ill,
> Why hath it given me earnest of success,
> Commencing in a truth ?—I am thane of Cawdor !
> If good, why do I yield to that suggestion
> Whose horrid image doth unfix my hair,
> And make my seated heart knock at my ribs,
> Against the use of nature ? "

> " Our fears in Banquo
> Stick deep; and in his royalty of nature
> Reigns that which would be feared; 'tis much he dares,
> And, to that dauntless temper of his mind,
> He hath a wisdom that doth guide his valour
> To act in safety.   There is none but he
> Whose being I do fear: and under him
> My genius is rebuked, as it is said
> Mark Antony's was by Cæsar.   He chid the sisters
> When first they put the name of king upon me,
> And bade them speak to him: then prophet-like
> They hailed him father to a line of kings;
> Upon my head they placed a fruitless crown,
> And put a barren sceptre in my gripe,
> Thence to be wrenched by an unlineal hand,
> No son of mine succeeding.   If 't be so,

For Banquo's issue have I 'filed my mind;
For them the gracious Duncan have I murdered;
Put rancours in the vessel of my peace
Only for them; and mine eternal jewel
Given to the common enemy of man,
To make them kings,—the seed of Banquo kings!
Rather than so, come, fate, into the list
And champion me to the utterance!"

"Time, thou anticipat'st my dread exploits:
The flighty purpose never is o'ertook,
Unless the deed go with it: from this moment,
The very firstlings of my heart shall be
The firstlings of my hand.   And even now
To crown my thoughts with acts, be it thought and done:
The castle of Macduff I will surprise;
Seize upon Fife; give to the edge o' the sword
His wife, his babes, and all unfortunate souls
That trace him in his line.   No boasting like a fool;
This deed I'll do before this purpose cool!"

" I have lived long enough; my way of life
Is fall'n into the sear, the yellow leaf;
And that which should accompany old age,
As honour, love, obedience, troops of friends,
I must not look to have; but in their stead
Curses not loud but deep, mouth-honour, breath
Which the poor heart would fain deny, but dares not."

The story of Macbeth, as related by Shakespeare, embraces I believe a lapse of twenty years.   In the first act he is introduced to us in lusty, early manhood, fit in limb as well as heart to breast the toil of war, and in the fifth act we find him " fall'n into the sear, the yellow leaf."

M

A life—a long life we might say—enacted in the space of some three hours. But who takes note of this? Where does the interest flag on this account? Is the horror of each succeeding deed of blood the less because minutes stand for the months or years that separated it from its precursor? When Macbeth tells us that he " has in blood stepp'd in so far that should he wade no more, returning were as tedious as go o'er"—do we breathe the less thick, because it was only a quarter of an hour ago that we saw him begin to wade ? If not, then what avails the unity of time or the unity of place ?

THE END.